The Bachelor
and the
Bean

Shelley Fowles

FRANCES LINCOLN

Once, long ago, there was a grumpy old bachelor who lived in a little town in Morocco.

One day, he bought a snack of cooked beans
in the market. But just before he could
finish it, the last bean dropped into a well.
"My bean, my bean!" he yelled.

An imp jumped out of the well.
"What **IS** all the fuss about?"
he asked.

"Give me back my bean!" the angry old bachelor shouted.

"By the hair of my grandmother's beard! It is only a miserable bean!" exclaimed the imp. "Look, here is a magic pot. Ask for whatever you want to eat, and it will appear. Only keep the noise down – I hate a racket!"

And with these words, the imp dived back into his well.

"Pot, give me a lovely stew with almonds
and raisins," said the bachelor, feeling a bit silly.
To his amazement, he got his wish: a delicious
stew appeared inside his new pot!

The bachelor showed the wonderful pot to all his neighbours, asking them to order whatever they pleased. They were thrilled and everyone was happy. Everyone, that is, except one jealous old lady.

"I'll come back tonight and swap it for one of my own," she thought. "He'll never notice!"

So that is what she did.

But the bachelor soon noticed that the pot
stayed empty when he asked it for food.

He went back to the well.

"Hey you! Imp!" the bachelor said rudely.
"Your pot doesn't work. It's worn out already.
Give me another one!"

The imp looked at the pot.

"This is not the pot I gave you, and I only had one like it. I'm not made of pots! Take this other one instead. Ask it for plates, cups, that sort of thing," he snapped, "and leave me alone!"

He dived back into the well with a bad-tempered splash.

The new pot proved to be even better than
the first one. It filled up with any vessels and plates
the bachelor asked for, and they were all of solid gold,
silver and crystal.

The bachelor was delighted, and told all his neighbours.

But once again, the jealous old lady stole his pot — only this time, she didn't bother to replace it.

The bachelor went back to the imp.

"You again!" the imp said grumpily.
"I heard what happened. People are talking
about it all over the market. Well, I have
one last pot for you. Fill it with water
and look inside – and don't come back!"

The old bachelor filled the pot with water
and gazed into it.
    Slowly a picture formed of the jealous old lady
with the stolen pots.

He rushed to her house and banged on the door.
"Give me back my pots, you old bag!"
A voice shrieked back at him, "Who are you
calling an old bag? You can't have the pots back.
They are mine now!"

The old bachelor was amazed. Such a strong voice!
Such a nasty temper! Such awful manners ...
What a wonderful woman! How they would shout
at each other! They were a perfect match.
  "**Marry me, you silly old bag**," he yelled,
"and then the pots will belong to both of us!"

So the grumpy old bachelor got his pots and
a wife. They had a huge wedding party with
food from one pot and tableware from the other.
    And from then on, I am happy to say, their
quarrels could be heard from one end of
the town to the other!